Books by Nancy Saxon
Illustrated by Charles Saxon

PANKY AND WILLIAM
PANKY IN THE SADDLE

Panky in
the Saddle

Panky in

by Nancy Saxon

ATHENEUM

the Saddle

illustrated by Charles Saxon

New York   1984

Library of Congress Cataloging in Publication Data

Saxon, Nancy.
Panky in the saddle.

Sequel to: Panky and William.
Summary: Panky learns a great deal from training William, an
unschooled pony, enough that she can accept inevitable changes
when her father loses his job.
[1. Ponies—Fiction]   I. Saxon, Charles D., ill.   II. Title.
PZ7.S27433Pam   1984   [Fic]   83-15910
ISBN 0-689-31038-2

To

Boris,
Duffy,
Lightfoot,
Bye-Bye,
Mr. Chips,
Dixie,
Stardust,
Cadeau,
Gracie,
Carrot Top,
Double or Nothing,
Cupcake
and Mister.

Panky in the Saddle

M Y J O U R N A L

NAME: Frances Mooney (everybody calls me Panky)

AGE: Almost eleven

EYES: Blue

HAIR: Dark brown

WEIGHT: I'll put that in later, when I'm completely back to normal.

ADDRESS: 243 Whiskey Lane, Old Forge, Conn.

RELATIVES: Mother and father at same address. They're OK as far as parents go, but they have a lot of problems.

FRIENDS: (1) *Katie Riley*. She's my best friend. Her father is head groom at Fox Run Hunt Club, so Katie knows all about horses.

(2) Tiffany Calder. She and her horse, Tiger Lily, are really good! Tiffany started riding in summer camp, and she got her own horse as soon as she joined Fox Run, so she is way ahead of me. Sometimes I think I'll never catch up with her!

(3) Melanie Smithers owns a pony named Cupcake. Melanie treats Cupcake like a big baby, but I have to admit he's cute.

(4) Caroline Horner rides in a class at Fox Run. She acts like she's afraid of her own horse.

(5) Hugo is the riding instructor at Fox Run. He's very strict and people find themselves doing things they didn't know they could do. I think Hugo's terrific!

(6) William is my favorite horse and my best friend who's not a person. I tell him everything, even if he can't understand. He used to be wild, but now he's calming down, thanks to me.

CLUBS OR ORGANIZATIONS: Fox Run Hunt Club. I used to think clubs were mean because somebody was always being left out. Then I decided it was silly of me to worry because I get left out plenty! The truth is, I have a very inferior feeling from time to time, like I'm not even a member of the human race. Belonging to a club ought to take that away, I think.

AMBITION IN LIFE: To be a GREAT horse-woman!

Chapter 1

OK, HERE GOES! I'm calling this a journal because I don't want to put something in it every day, the way you do with a diary. I only want to write what's important, and what's important to me is everything about learning to ride. I've decided that horses are going to be my life.

Until I met Katie, I dreamed about horses and drew pictures of them, but that's as far as it went. I never even saw a live horse, much less got on one. Then I got to know Katie at school, and she knows a lot about horses because her father is head groom at Fox Run Hunt Club. That's where I'm learning to ride.

The other kids didn't have much to do with me until Katie. Maybe it's because of the way I look. I have this weight problem. Maybe I ought to come right out and say it. I'm fat, and I used to be fatter. I guess I ate because I wasn't having much fun.

Katie noticed me because of the pictures I drew of horses. One day, she invited me to see the horses at Fox Run, and that's how I met William. Katie said he was what some people call a real mean horse, but I never called him that. I loved him at first sight. It didn't matter to me that his coat was shaggy and dirty or that his mane was full of straw. He had beautiful, sorrowful eyes, and I could see he was just plain lonesome. He looked the way I felt most of the time.

Katie said the club might have to get rid of William because nobody wanted to ride him. Most people at Fox Run own their own horses, but a few of them, like me, have to rent club horses by the hour. Nobody would use William because he bit and kicked everybody who went near his stall.

Poor William! He was so misunderstood! I started going to the stables every chance I could get, so he'd know he had a friend. When nobody was around, I sang to him. He would stare over my shoulder with a melancholy look in his eyes, as if he were dreaming of faraway things, like maybe the way it used to be before he got taken away from his mother.

After he got used to me, I went into his stall and combed the tangles out of his mane and tail. Nobody would believe it, but he never did the least little thing that was mean.

Anyway, Hugo, he's the riding instructor, found me one day in William's stall, and somehow, he and my parents got together and agreed to let me take lessons. That was pretty nice of my parents because they aren't the least bit interested in horses.

Over here at Fox Run, everybody is horse crazy, like me. For example, one day at a show a horse ran away and knocked down a tent, and a policeman came up and said, "How are you people?" Hugo stared at him and said, "If you had any sense, you'd say, 'How is the horse?' "

That's what I mean. At Fox Run, the horse comes first!

At home, all my daddy does is worry about the future of the steel industry. Daddy's an engineer who works for a steel company, and business is so bad, Daddy won't even let Mother buy a foreign car. He says he's not going to have foreign steel sitting in his driveway. And Mother's gotten so nervous, she cries at the least little thing.

In my opinion, their biggest problem is this house. Ever since we moved in, things have been breaking down. The people who sold it to us must have been rotten! They painted the house white, inside and out, so you couldn't see where all the leaks were. Mother blamed Daddy for buying the house. She said, being an engineer, he should have seen through all that white paint. He said he wasn't that kind of engineer, but she wouldn't listen. Then he said, "All right, I was wrong. I apologize to the whole world!" And Mother said, "Well, there's no point in being negative!"

They argue a lot these days. Most of the time, I try not to listen. I look at television and pretend not to hear. If they see me, they put on this phony, cheerful act and it's awful!

Now that I have horses to think about, things are better. A whole new world is opening up for me at Fox Run.

I want to be a great horsewoman! I hope by the end of this journal, I can tell about how William and I went to the National Horse Show at Madison Square Garden and won first prize. I can just see how it will be! We'll come prancing out in the spotlight to get the silver cup, and the whole place will be thundering with applause. Maybe William will take a bow, sort of going down on his front knees. Or maybe I'll say a few words on the microphone, thanking the people who helped me be a success. On the other hand, I may decide to give all the credit to William. I'd like to make up for the bad things that have happened to him.

When the time comes, I'm going to look a lot more like Tiffany than I do now. I'll be thin, and I'll wear yellow stretch pants and a yellow vest and a black jacket and derby. That's the way I've seen Tiffany dress for a fancy show.

The silver cup will be the happy ending of this journal, but tomorrow is the beginning, because I'm having my very first lesson!

I can't wait!

Chapter 2

WHEN MOTHER put me out at Fox Run, I stood for a moment before going inside. The truth is, I felt something close to stage fright. Maybe it's easier to dream about things than it is to get them. I'd been dreaming about horses for as long as I could remember and now, finally, I was going to ride one, and something held me back. Maybe, deep down, I wasn't crazy about the idea of riding at a fancy club. Fox Run isn't exactly a place where you poke around the old corral wearing chaps and a cowboy hat!

Furthermore, I'd picked the coldest day of the year to start out. A crust of snow smothered the roof of the red barn, and icicles, fierce as shark's teeth, hung off the edges. A few horses were out in the paddocks, snorting like dragons as they reared and nipped and chased. I knew they were just having fun, but there was something ferocious about them just the same. I really don't like to see a horse standing on his hind legs!

"What's the matter?" said Mother, rolling down the car window.

"I can't go in dressed like this," I said. "Everybody else will be dressed in proper riding clothes!"

I didn't want to say I was scared. Anyway, I DID look awful. I stood there, shivering in thin jeans and a pea-green sweater topped by Daddy's old golf jacket. The jacket was screaming, fire-engine red. I was about as quiet and tailored as a Christmas tree!

Mother frowned. "But you're a MEMBER now," she said, "and you have just as much right to be here as anybody else."

She sounded irritable. She gets that way when she's worried about money, which is practically all the time. What she was thinking was that she'd paid good money for me to become a junior member, and the least I could do was cooperate.

"Go on in and take your lesson," she said, impatiently. "We'll see about clothes later."

She settled the matter by snapping the window shut and driving away.

Icy wind bit down inside my collar, nudging me inside. I used both hands to slide the heavy barn door sideways and stepped inside. Right away, the wonderful smell of horses and hay and leather hit me. I knew then, without a doubt, that this was where I wanted to be. I really am crazy about horses! I looked down the aisle at a row of them, all hanging their heads out to see who was coming. I knew some of them, just to pet. Cupcake, Melanie Smithers's spoiled little pony, began to kick the boards of his stall, demanding attention. He gets plenty from Melanie, but it's never enough.

I ran past him and flung open the gate to William's stall. If horses could smile, William would have been snickering with delight. His soft brown eyes had lights in

them, and his ears were trimmed politely forward like sides of a clothespin. He didn't care if I looked like Mother Hubbard! I scratched him behind the ears, the way he likes it, and he rubbed his head against my shoulder.

I wouldn't even be in Fox Run if it weren't for William! He's the cutest horse I ever saw, with a soot black coat and thick, fringed eyelashes and a tail and mane that just wouldn't stop growing, even when the rest of him stayed small.

"Don't worry," I said, "we're going to have a good time."

I was sorry to shut the gate on him, but I figured I'd be back soon enough.

I found Hugo teaching a class in the indoor ring. The ring was oval-shaped with benches on one side. I sat down on a bench to watch. The clock on the wall said fifteen minutes of ten. My lesson was at ten.

Hugo was barking out orders like a general commanding an army. There's something about Hugo's voice that makes you jump, even if you're not on a horse. He was standing in the center of the ring, glaring at horses and riders as if willing them to do his bidding. I don't know why, but already I care a lot what Hugo thinks of me. That's the effect he has on people. Maybe it's because he knows everything there is to know about horses. He's gotten so bowlegged, his boots stand up straight even when his feet are planted wide apart.

I watched him stamp his feet to keep them from freezing. He never took his eyes off the horses. Boy! He really believes in discipline.

Katie peered around the corner, looking for me, I guess. If I were drawing Katie, I'd use my orange crayon for her hair and a brown crayon with a sharp point for her freckles. I'd have to make about a million dots because that's how many freckles she has. Her eyes were bright green under a black hunt cap, and she had her hands stuffed into a ball-shaped jacket.

"Panky!" she said. "Are you here for a lesson?"

I nodded, grinning. There was no point

pretending to be cool with Katie. She knew how excited I was.

"Come on!" she said. "Let's go to the office and see who you're riding."

"What about William?" I asked.

Katie's eyes widened. "My goodness!" she said. "You can't ride William! He's not a beginner horse, not by a long shot!"

I felt really let down. I'd just assumed William and I would start together.

"Maybe you can ride him later on," said Katie. "You aren't going to stay a beginner."

The office was on the other side of the wall with the clock. Katie introduced me to a Miss B, a lady who looked like a nice, old horse. She even had a way of ducking her head to one side, as if she were peering down a long horse nose at you.

She pumped my hand with a fierce grip.

"Nice to have you here, Panky," she said, sizing me up with a sideways look. "Done any riding?"

I had to say no.

"Then we'd better put you on Boris," she said. "He's an old professor of a horse. He'll take good care of you."

She picked up a telephone connected to the stable.

"Saddle up Boris," she said, "and bring him around to the mounting block."

My heart started pounding. I was actually going to get up on a horse!

Katie grabbed my hand, and we ran to meet Boris. On the way, we bumped into Katie's father. He had Katie's red hair and the same friendly grin.

"Whoa, there!" he said, swinging Katie around in a hug. "Don't you know better than to run in a stable? Scares the horses!"

"This is Panky's first lesson" said Katie.

"Well, don't let me hold you up," said her father, waving us away. "Good luck, Panky!"

He strode off down the aisle. I noticed he wore brown boots like Hugo's only they weren't as shiny.

"I'll tell you a secret," said Katie. "My father has gypsy blood in him. That's why he's so good with horses."

That meant Katie was good with horses too. Well, so was I, even if I didn't have gypsy blood.

The mounting block was a small platform with two steps up and two steps down. I bounded up the steps just as the groom arrived with Boris. Katie had taught me how to groom a horse on Boris because he was easy. But he was probably the homeliest horse in the stable, even to a horse lover. His nose ran in a curved line to a point under his chin, and his coat was dull black and brown, like a mule. He even had big, mule-like ears. The worst thing was his size. He was huge!

"Don't worry," said Katie. "He may be big, but he's the safest horse in the stable."

Katie showed me how to hold the reins in my left hand and swing my leg over the saddle. When my feet were in the stirrups, Katie led Boris to the gate and opened it for us. Boris made a blubbering sound with his lips.

My heart stopped.

"What's he doing?" I asked.

Katie grinned. "He says he likes you."

I didn't think Katie was being funny. It was a long way to the ground, and I wasn't in control anymore. I wondered if there was any truth to the saying that horses can smell fear. It was one of those things you couldn't ask. It would sound dumb.

Hugo saw me and smiled a welcome, and I tried to smile back. There were two other girls in the ring, and they were dressed in neat jodhpurs, hunt caps, and jackets filled with warm goosedown.

One of the girls was Tiffany West. She's the person in my class at school who does everything first, like braiding strands of plastic in her hair and wearing shoe laces with designs on them. She looked even better on a horse than she did walking around. Her blonde hair hung in a braid down her back, and she was riding a pretty gray horse with dappled spots and a white mane and tail. I thought it must be an Arabian. That's the prettiest horse there is.

Tiffany nodded coolly as if she hardly knew me, let alone rode on the bus to school with me every day. The other girl was named Caroline Horner, and I didn't mind her being unfriendly because I didn't know her. She has a cold, haughty expression, as if she doesn't care to associate with people who wear old golf jackets. I tried not to take it personally. There's no law that says people have to like me.

Hugo told them to introduce their mounts, and Tiffany broke into a smile and said her horse's name was Tiger Lily. Caroline's horse was named Dixie. I could tell Tiffany was proud of Tiger Lily. Well, I'd be proud too if I were on William.

Hugo said I was going to share their lesson, even though I was a beginner. He said I could learn a lot watching more experienced riders. I wondered if he were trying to help me make friends. I'm kind of sensitive about that. Anyway, if that's what he had in mind, it didn't work. Tiffany and Caroline weren't one bit glad to have me share their lesson. I think they pretended I wasn't even there.

Before we could get started, Katie came in on a horse. She sort of crashed through the gate, and her horse started galloping right away. Caroline's horse let out a high-pitched squeak and bounced up in the air.

"You'd better join us," Hugo said to Katie. "Fall in line with the others."

I was amazed that Katie couldn't control her horse. I'd thought she was good. For some reason, Hugo didn't tell her anything. Instead, he came over to me and fixed the reins in my hands, turning the fists in a thumbs up position.

"Heels down, shoulders back," he said. "And the reins should be a straight line from the elbow to the bit."

I sneaked a look at Tiffany. Her reins were perfect.

Hugo said the first thing we would work on was getting the horse to walk properly. He wanted us to walk briskly, keeping the horse's head up and making him pick up his feet.

"Caroline," he snapped. "Get a better walk on that horse! Where do you think you are, the Lazy U Ranch?"

We had to circle the ring three times before he was satisfied. Then he said, "Now ladies, trot, please!"

The other girls started posting, going up and down in rhythm to the horse. I tried to do what they did, but all I did was bounce! Boris had a long, loping post. When I came down too soon, I got spanked, hard, by the saddle. I tried to slow my movements to match Boris. I was still up in the air when Hugo said, "Half the ring!"

Boris turned sharply, following Dixie's lead. I came down on the side of the saddle and lost my balance. The next thing I knew, I was sliding past Boris's huge belly, and then I was on the ground. I landed on my shoulder and rolled over twice. Then I just sat there. Sawdust was in my mouth, and Daddy's red jacket was caked with dirt.

I thought, "So this is the end of the great horsewoman!"

Hugo was there in a second, checking for sprains or fractures and helping me to my feet.

"Well, you certainly know how to fall!" he said. "You rolled like an acrobat!"

He turned to the class. "Every horsewoman should know how to fall properly. It happens to all of us."

I thought I saw an expression of con-

tempt on Tiffany's face. I couldn't blame her. I wasn't hurt, but I could have died of shame!

Boris was standing at a respectful distance, reins dangling. Hugo led him over, made a low stirrup of his hands for me to step in, and lifted me onto Boris's back.

"Grip with your knees," he said, pressing my leg against Boris's side as if gluing it in place. "Make your legs a vise. You never know when your horse will make a sudden move."

He told us to trot, and I started going up and down, but my legs were too weak to grip anything. I could feel I was doing everything wrong.

"Panky, your reins are flying all over the place!" said Hugo. "When you wave your arms like that, you're telling your horse to go."

He was all business. Maybe it was better that way. I didn't want pity. I curled my little finger under the neck rein to steady my hands. It worked.

"That's better," said Hugo.

I tried to remember everything I'd been

told. Heels down, shoulders back. Straight line from the elbow to the bit. Keep the horse's head up, but don't come back on his mouth. There were too many things to think of at once. I must have drooped in defeat, because Hugo watched me, frowning. When I passed by him, he said in a low voice, "Sit up straight! It's terrible when a girl doesn't sit up straight!"

I tried to square my shoulders and went on bouncing. Luckily, Boris seemed to understand everything Hugo was saying. When Hugo said, "Trot," he did it without me telling him to.

By the end of the lesson, I was beginning to appreciate him. Then he went and spoiled everything. When the clock said eleven, he ambled into the middle of the ring, firmly planted his big hooves, and refused to take another step.

Tiffany gave Caroline a meaningful glance.

"Boris can tell time," Caroline said with what I thought was a superior smile. "He knows you only paid for one hour."

I shook the reins and clucked, which I know you're not supposed to do. I was getting frantic. Boris didn't budge.

The others started laughing, Katie too, and I felt myself turning red. Hugo rescued me by leading Boris out to the mounting block.

"Next week, I'll show you how to handle this," he said. "You've had enough for one day."

I'll say I'd had enough! I felt as if I'd been run over by a truck! But the worst thing was the way I felt inside. I was ashamed of myself, through and through. I'd fallen off the beginner horse, and everybody had laughed at how dumb I was.

"It's not easy, Panky," said Hugo, kindly. "But if you're willing to work, I'll teach you how to ride. Are you going to stick with it?"

I knew if I looked at him, I'd cry.

"Yes," I said, keeping my eyes on the ground. I added a mumbled, "Thanks."

Mother was waiting in the car.

"My goodness!" she said. "You sure are walking funny, Panky!"

I sank carefully into the seat, wondering if I had any broken bones. My hands had blisters on them where the reins had rubbed them raw. They don't wear those gloves just to look good.

"Did you enjoy your lesson?" said Mother, beginning to look worried. "Are you sure you like riding?"

I knew I couldn't quit. If I wasn't a horsewoman, I was nothing!

"Sure!" I said, pretending a confidence I didn't feel. "I want all the lessons I can get!"

Chapter 3

WHEN I SHOWED UP for my second lesson, I checked in at the office and found Miss B on the telephone and Caroline Horner standing by her with her back to me.

"We're trying out that new chestnut," Miss B was saying. "Hugo says he's a handful. He wants to put Katie on him and see what she thinks."

Suddenly, I understood about Katie. She was good, all right. She was so good, Hugo put her on problem horses to help school them. I was glad, because, next to Hugo, Katie's teaching me most about horses.

As soon as Miss B got off the telephone, Caroline started begging to ride Boris.

"I need him more than Panky!" she pleaded.

"But you have a horse," said Miss B. "What would your mother say if you didn't ride Dixie?"

Caroline looked desperate.

"I never know what Dixie's going to do next!" she said. "Just the least little thing, and she goes to pieces. Like the other day, a paper cup blew down from the bleachers, and she reared!"

"She's quick," Miss B admitted. "She's a high-strung, Thoroughbred mare. But if you reach the point where you can control her, she'll be more fun than any club horse!"

"I don't care," said Caroline, miserably. "Couldn't I just walk her around for exercise?"

"You're not supposed to be walking," said Miss B patiently. "You're supposed to be riding. Besides," she added, "you're not a beginner, like Panky."

Caroline suddenly realized I was there and looked embarrassed.

"Oh, all right," she said, giving up and moving towards the door.

I was shocked. What I had thought was a cold, arrogant expression was a mask covering up fear. I almost felt sorry for her.

I told Katie about it when we were in the ring. Katie explained that Caroline's mother used to hunt down in Virginia, and she wanted Caroline to have the same kind of fun she'd had. Katie added in a whisper. "I don't think Caroline even likes horses!"

That seemed like a real shame with so many people wanting and needing horses.

I was sort of glad to see Tiffany ride in as if she owned the place. I admire her confidence, even though Katie had told me Tiger Lily is what you call a 'made' horse. That is, she was already trained when Tiffany got her. I don't care. I still think Tiffany has style. Like today, she was wearing a yellow turtle-necked sweater and she'd tied a matching yellow ribbon on Tiger's tail. No matter what Tiffany's wearing, you get the feeling she's in technicolor and everybody else is black and white.

"I wish I looked like that," I said, thinking out loud. "I mean I wish I had a turtle-necked sweater," I added quickly. "It looks warm."

"It ought to be," said Katie. "Tiffany's sweaters are cashmere. Her mother orders them from England."

I didn't have time to think about that because Hugo started the lesson.

We were working on our walk again. Hugo wanted it to be PERFECT.

"Wibrate! Wibrate!" he shouted.

Katie giggled. Hugo grew up in Germany, and sometimes he has an accent.

Hugo tried again.

"Vibrate! Vibrate!" he said. "If you want good hands, you have to get a feel of the horse's mouth."

He saw I was confused.

"When Boris is walking," he asked me, "does he hold his head still?"

I said no.

"Then don't hold your hands still," said Hugo. "Your hands should respond to the movement of the horse's head. And keep a firm contact, or he'll stumble."

It made sense, but it was one more thing to remember.

I tried hard to do everything right, and I could see I was improving. I didn't bounce nearly as high on the post as I did before. But I still didn't know what I'd do when Boris decided to call it quits. And he did, promptly at eleven. Whatever instinct it is that tells horses these things notified him that the hour was up. He headed for the center of the ring, neatly settled his hooves in place, and turned to stone!

The others had been waiting for this, and they watched to see what I would do. I jabbed Boris with my heels, getting madder and madder. I wanted to cluck and throw my reins around, but I didn't. Still, how do you make a mountain move?

Hugo handed me a crop.

"Squeeze with your legs," he said. "At the same time, hit him with this."

I fluttered the crop weakly against Boris' hindquarters.

"Don't give him a lot of little taps," said Hugo, sternly. "Hit him once and make it count!"

I squeezed with my legs and whacked Boris with the crop, HARD!

The mountain ambled back to the wall and fell into an easy trot.

"Now, halt," said Hugo.

I sat back and pulled the reins.

Boris stopped.

"That's the whole idea," said Hugo. "He goes when you say go. He halts when you say halt."

His face relaxed into a crinkled grin.

"Class dismissed," he said. "Nice work, Panky!"

I forgot that I was the worst rider in the class and that my clothes were all wrong. Suddenly, I felt wonderful.

Chapter 4

WHEN DADDY asked me how the riding was coming along, I told him how I'd shown Boris who was boss. I was sort of bragging, but the part about hitting Boris didn't sound so good. I don't want people to think I beat horses!

It didn't matter because Daddy didn't notice.

"Do the other girls use club horses?" he asked.

I told him Katie and I were the only junior riders who didn't own a horse. Daddy's face collapsed into his St. Bernard look.

"Why do they have club horses," he said, gloomily, "if nobody rides them?"

"Members rent them for their guests," I

explained. "And most people start out on club horses. When they get good, they usually buy a horse from Hugo."

Daddy still looked worried.

"Well, the least we can do is fix you up with proper clothes," he said. "I'm taking back my golf jacket."

That was good news. If I never see that red jacket again, it's too soon!

Mother was in no hurry to take me shopping, even when Daddy told her to. She's really got a hang-up about money these days. She says things like, "Well, at least group lessons are cheaper than private lessons." When she wanted me to take dancing lessons, she wasn't like that.

I waited until after I'd had four more lessons on Boris. Then I made an all-out effort.

"Look," I said, sticking my finger down inside my belt to show how much room there was. "I'm down a whole size, and I think I'm going to stay this way for a while. Maybe even lose some more. How about buying me some real riding pants?"

Mother looked at my waistline with approval.

"You know, I think you have lost weight," she said.

I wasn't just thinner. I was different. A lot of baby fat had turned into muscle, especially in my legs. I wasn't just a big blob anymore. I was really getting in shape, and I owed it all to riding.

"You know, it's not just snob stuff or wanting to be like everybody else," I said. "With riding clothes, there's a reason for everything. Jodhpurs have a suede liner so the stirrups won't rub the insides of your legs. The helmet keeps your brains from getting scrambled in case you fall. Even a stock has a purpose. You can use it as a sling if you break your arm."

I hoped I hadn't overdone the danger part.

"Horses are all I care about," I said.

"That's a fact," said Mother. "Well, your father is right. It's time to buy you a proper riding outfit. We certainly want you to look as nice as everybody else."

She took me to a shop near Fox Run where everything was for the horse and rider. The pictures on the walls were hunting scenes, and there were little horse statues for sale and horseshoe ashtrays and belts with fox heads on them. It was a neat store. I could spend a fortune in a place like that!

I settled for stretch pants, a brown tweed jacket, a brown hunt cap, new gloves, and a yellow neck band like one I'd seen Tiffany wear.

I was sitting on a wooden horse to check the fit of my pants when Melanie came in.

"Hi, Panky," she greeted me. "Mother's given me fifteen minutes to buy Cupcake a new blanket. Then she's picking me up."

She wasted no time selecting a standard blue plaid blanket and charging it. Then, when her mother didn't come, she came over to talk.

"Mother's always forgetting about me," she said. "I wouldn't mind, but I hate being away from Cupcake. He gets lonesome."

"At least you're buying something for him," I said.

"That's right," said Melanie. "It's for his own good."

As long as she had time, she decided to buy brushes and a few more grooming tools. All she does is groom Cupcake, so I guess things wear out.

Mother offered to give her a ride home, but Melanie said she'd better wait for her mother. She was still charging things when we left.

As soon as I got home, I put on my new clothes. I polished the boots I'd gotten for Christmas and put them on last. When I looked in the mirror, I couldn't help grinning. I looked on the outside the way I felt on the inside.

For the next few days, as soon as I got home from school, I put on my new riding clothes. I took them off to sleep, but that's all.

What I wanted to do was go right over to Fox Run and show off the way I looked, but I had to wait until my next lesson. Not that I'd make much of a flap! I wouldn't look any better or any worse than anybody else, but so what! They look good.

I spent the time making out a list of things I was supposed to remember, like "heels down, shoulders back" and all that stuff. I didn't bother writing down the chief thing I'd learned, which was respect for Boris. He was as good a horse as you were a rider. The better you got, the better Boris acted. Everybody knew this, and that's why they'd laughed when Boris quit on me that first day when my hour was up. Well, they wouldn't laugh now!

Sometimes, except for Katie, I felt as if my new friends at Fox Run were a bunch of rich snobs, and I wanted to show them who the REAL rider was. Other times, like now, I was glad to be exactly like them!

OK. So now I look like a horsewoman. I feel like a horsewoman. I hope I'm beginning to ride like one.

The next step has to be William!

Chapter 5

HUGO WASN'T enthusiastic, but I wore him down. I reminded him he'd as good as promised me I could ride William before I started taking lessons.

"All right," he said, finally, "but if it doesn't work out, you go back to Boris."

Katie added her warning.

"William's not going to be a little lamb when you get on his back!"

I guess I was the only one who knew William wouldn't hurt me. Why would he want to kill off the only friend he had?

When I came over for the big lesson, Hugo was giving William a workout in the pony ring. He had William on a lunge line, which is sort of like a long dog leash, and he was running him in circles. Every time William stopped, Hugo cracked a whip in the air to make him run again. Poor old William was covered with lather! When he was ready to drop in his tracks, Hugo said, "I think he's ready for you, Panky."

The groom led William out to the mounting block, and he stood there looking pitiful with his head hanging down to his knees. I swung my leg carefully over the saddle, afraid he might collapse under my weight.

Then a funny thing happened. Suddenly, William wasn't tired anymore! He started prancing around and tossing his head in an excited way.

"Hey!" I patted him on the neck. "Remember me? I'm Panky!"

He jumped as if I'd scared him, and I hurriedly got my hands back in position. I might as well be on a strange horse. He even looked different from the top.

Hugo opened the gate for us.

"You're not on Boris," he reminded me unnecessarily.

William's muscles were bunched up, and I had a sinking feeling he might buck.

I looked around for Katie and Tiffany.

They were sitting at a safe distance in the stands. Even Melanie had managed to tear herself away from Cupcake to watch. Today, I was all by myself!

"Trot, please," said Hugo.

I squeezed my legs, and William shot straight up in the air! I flew out of the saddle, and when I came back down, Hugo calmly repeated the command.

This time, William broke into a run. I decided one of his ancestors must have been a racehorse. Maybe not one who came in first, but not one with tired blood either.

"Sit back!" Hugo ordered.

I tried to sit back, but I wasn't exactly relaxed.

"Turn him in a circle," said Hugo.

I tried, only it was more of a triangle than a circle.

"Halt!" Hugo boomed.

With a few nasty little bounces, we came to a halt. I knew what Hugo was doing because I'd seen Katie do the same thing with difficult horses. He was giving orders so thick and fast, William wouldn't have time to think what HE wanted to do!

"Now, trot," said Hugo.

William was off again in a flat-out gallop.

"Sit back! Sit back!" Hugo shouted.

I didn't even try. It was all I could do to keep from throwing my arms around William's neck.

I caught a flying glimpse of Katie and the others watching from their safe perch in the bleachers. How I wished I could trade places with them! The awful truth is, when you're in trouble on a horse, nobody can help you.

Hugo shouted, "Half the ring!"

I tugged on the left rein, and William cut off a slice of the ring. Some of the steam was going out of him.

"Halt!" said Hugo.

William slowed down, probably because he felt like it, and Hugo grabbed hold of the bridle.

"When you say halt and mean business," he said, keeping an iron grip on William, "keep your left hand steady and yank hard on the right hand. Like this." He jerked the right rein. "Pull it up high so he feels it."

The next time William bolted, I tried it. It worked. William was as surprised as I was.

"That little horse needs discipline," said Hugo. "He won't be worth a plugged nickel without it."

I managed to carry out a few more orders, but, fortunately, the lesson was nearing the end.

Hugo said, "Well, now, I think we're getting somewhere."

I sagged weakly off of William onto the mounting block. My legs had as much strength as overcooked spaghetti. I just made it, leading William to his stall. I was really beat! William had acted like a wild horse, just what everybody said he was. He was a different animal in the ring from the one who stood quietly and let me groom him. The knowledge gradually sank into me. I knew that from now on, I had to treat him more like a horse than a person.

There was something sad about it. I felt

as if I'd lost a friend. It had been fun talking to him and singing when we were by ourselves. Now, I wondered if he'd ever really liked my songs.

Tiffany and Katie and Melanie came over and stood silently, watching me rub him down. I made myself do a careful job of getting all the sweat off.

"Wow!" said Katie. "That was some lesson! I've got to hand it to you, Panky. You've got guts!"

"Thanks," I said. I didn't say so, but Hugo was the one with guts. He had brainwashed me into following orders, and I had brainwashed William.

"I'll say one thing for Cupcake," said Melanie. "He's not mean."

"William's not mean," I said. "He just likes to have his own way. All he needs is training."

"I don't see how you can train him when you ride just one day a week," said Tiffany.

Neither did I, but I didn't like her saying it.

They walked away, and I turned back

to William. He was chomping hay as if he didn't know I existed.

I was getting that old, left-out feeling. The way Tiffany and Melanie acted, you'd think I wasn't even a member of the club. And I wasn't too happy about seeing Katie walking off with them. You'd think she'd want to hang around. Katie must have guessed how I felt because she suddenly turned and called back.

"He could have bucked you off easy if he'd wanted to, Panky. He really does like you."

I wasn't sure of that.

Chapter 6

"PANKY! I've got the answer!" Katie yelled. She didn't care who was listening. "I've got the answer to your problem!"

It so happened I was standing in the cafeteria line picking up a saucer with a slab of chocolate cake on it.

I let the saucer drop with a clatter. Once you've had a weight problem, you have a tendency to feel guilty about things.

"Excuse me! Excuse me!" Katie said, trying to push her way through the line. She gave up and called, "Hold a seat for me, Panky!"

When we were settled with our lunch trays, Katie started in at once.

"You know how William needs to be trained and you don't have time to do it?"

"Uh, huh," I mumbled, biting into a hot dog.

"Well, if you could just take him on board, you could ride him every day for as long as you wanted to! I'm sure Hugo wouldn't mind if your father is willing. All he'll pay the club is what it costs to keep William."

I turned the idea over in my mind. When I first started riding, I would have jumped at the chance to ride William every day. Now that I knew a thing or two, I was more cautious.

"How can I train William," I said, "when I'm not even trained myself? What IS training anyway?"

"You've already started," Katie said. "Training a horse is a matter of doing everything right. Horses have phenomenal memories, and you can't make many mistakes. But don't worry. Hugo will help you. So will I," she added.

Katie knew almost as much about horses as Hugo. With both of them to help me, it might be possible.

"Take a chance!" said Katie, her green eyes bright with excitement. "What have you got to lose?"

Nothing as it turned out. I wasn't crazy enough to ask Mother. You'd think the way she acts, we're ready for the poorhouse. I caught Daddy when he was in a good humor, and he didn't need any persuading at all.

So I took William on board, which, for practical purposes, was almost as good as owning him.

Riding him every day made all the difference! His progress was phenomenal! And I got as tough as a professional athlete. I probably could wrestle a crocodile to death with my bare legs! I needed strong leg muscles to hang on to William in case he came up with any surprises.

I could see William was strong and he'd always like to lead the parade, that was his nature, but I think he liked having rules. He calmed down in a hurry. I tried to do everything right and consistently, and William responded. He was suddenly living in a world with rewards and punishments. Also, like Katie said, part of his trouble had been lack of exercise.

Katie said for a while I'd have to concentrate all the time on doing the right thing, but after a while, I'd do things right automatically. She said the same thing went for William. But she warned me that horses can get untrained even after a lot of work has gone into training them.

On Sunday, I had a chance to see what she meant. I went over to Fox Run after Sunday school, which landed me there about eleven fifteen. The indoor ring was full of grown people. They sat way back in their saddles and rode sort of stiffly, showing off how great they were at dressage. Some of them were dressed in derbies with white stocks and white gloves and they nodded formally to each other and said "Good morning! Isn't it a lovely day?" even though it was lousy outside.

I noticed one horse was wearing pads around his ankles and hanging his head in a miserable, hangdog way.

I cantered around the ring a few times to take the steam out of William, then I sidled up to Katie.

"What's the matter with that bay?" I asked. "Did he hurt his ankles?"

Katie shook her head. "He kicks himself!" she said.

Boy! That was really dumb, even for a horse!

The horse raised his head for a moment, and I noticed a slender, proud arch to his neck.

"Hey! Is he a Thoroughbred?" I asked.

Katie nodded.

"I'll tell you a secret," she whispered, walking so close our horses were scraping sides. "That horse costs twenty thousand dollars!"

I looked to see who could pay that kind of money. Mrs. Martin was riding her. She wasn't anybody's mother, and I just saw her on Sundays. She looked like an advertisement or something, except for the way her horse was hanging his head and shuffling along. Thoroughbred or not, he might as well have been pulling a plow.

"What happened?" I asked.

"Hugo brought the horse up from Southern Pines," said Katie, "and he had me ride the horse every day for a couple of weeks. Then one day, he had me run through his gaits for Mrs. Martin. She liked what she saw and bought the horse. Her idea was to win ribbons in the local shows and have everybody think she was a great rider." Katie paused. "The trouble is, she's not very good." Katie said it almost apologetically. "I never saw a horse go downhill so fast! I couldn't believe it when he started kicking himself! You should see the rubber bells they put on his hooves when he's turned out!"

For the life of me I couldn't see what Mrs. Martin was doing wrong.

"He's a horse that has to be collected," said Katie. "If you don't drive him onto the bit with your legs, he stumbles."

As if to prove her point, the horse stumbled, shaking Mrs. Martin out of her Sunday morning look.

"You see," said Katie. "I'd offer to exercise him, but she's too proud to let me. Why is it," Katie sighed, "that so many people want to think they're the greatest thing in the world on a horse?"

Seeing as I'm one of them, I felt kind of sorry for Mrs. Martin. It must be terrible to pay a fortune for a horse and have him hang his head and kick himself!

"Wouldn't you rather be somebody who took a horse that wasn't," she hesitated, picking her words carefully, "valuable," she said, "and made something out of him than somebody who pays a fortune for a 'made' horse and untrains him?"

I didn't have a fortune to spend on a horse, but the answer would have been the same even if I had. I was on him.

Chapter 7

HUGO'S THE ONE WHO persuaded me
to sign up for the club show. He was en-
couraging everybody to enter. "It's just a
small family show," he said. "It doesn't matter whether you win anything or not. It will
be good experience for William."

Our first show! Hugo had no idea how
important this was to me. Maybe I should
know better by now, but I still have dreams
of glory. Later on, if William and I win the
silver cup at Madison Square Garden, I'll re-
mind Hugo of the day he asked me to enter
my first show.

I signed up for 'walk, trot, canter,' fig-
uring I'd learn how to canter before the
show. It turned out to be easy. We were out
in the field one day, down at the far end,

and when we started back to the barn, William broke into a canter. It was not a run or his usual speedy trot, but a nice, easy, rocking horse canter. It felt wonderful!

Hugo was watching, and when we got back, he said, "Whose idea was that?" I said, "Ours," and Hugo laughed. I guess he knows it will be a long time before all the ideas are mine.

After that, we cantered all the time. Sometimes, William got bored cantering in the ring. Hugo told me to push with my seat, as if I were pumping in a swing, to keep him going.

I wasn't the only one getting ready for the show. Tiffany was having a lesson almost every day. I heard her asking Katie how many points you needed to compete for the McClay. That's the most important trophy there is for a junior rider. If Tiffany sets out to win it, she probably will. There can't be many riders who look as good as she does on Tiger Lily.

Katie was schooling horses for other people to show. She's always exercising

other people's horses. On a really cold day,
when people don't feel like coming over, she
rides one horse after another. Sometimes,
she brings the horses into our lessons, but
it's just because Hugo likes her. I don't think
she pays. Poor Katie! She's sort of a Cinderella, doing all the work to make other people
look good. The difference between her and
Cinderella is that you can't feel sorry for
Katie, because she doesn't feel sorry for herself. She says she learns more by riding a lot
of different horses than if she rode just one.

Melanie shocked everybody by riding
Cupcake into the ring one day. We tried not
to laugh, but she really did look funny. Her
feet were almost touching the ground. Then,
when she tried to make Cupcake trot, he
stumbled and fell flat on his face. He stood
up and blinked in a dazed sort of way, his
white face all spattered with dirt. Naturally,
Melanie wasn't hurt. Right away, she started
consoling Cupcake and telling him he was a
good boy. She reached into her pocket to
get a lump of sugar, and that's when Katie
swooped down on them.

"That's enough!" she said, sternly. "Don't you dare reward that horse for falling, or he'll do it over and over again!"

Melanie put the sugar back in her pocket. I couldn't imagine him falling down to get attention, but it's probably true. Katie gave me a hard look to see if I was noticing. I got the message. Horses have long memories, and it's as easy to untrain them as it is to train them.

It's too bad she couldn't have taught that to Melanie. Everybody knows Cupcake's gotten so greedy for sugar, he's turned into a nipper.

After that, Melanie announced that she wouldn't ride Cupcake in the show, but she'd walk him around to watch so he wouldn't feel left out.

Caroline sort of shrinks if you mention show, so nobody talks about it to her.

As far as I was concerned, everybody was readier than I was. I asked Hugo if there was any way I could catch up with the others. He said the only shortcut he knew was to practice sit trotting without stirrups. I practically bounced my insides out, but I did it every day. Soon, my legs began to hang in a more natural position, and I didn't lean forward as much. Katie said I was getting a good seat.

William was improving, too.

"He's learning," said Hugo. "It just shows you can teach a calf if you work at it."

Hugo's a snob about breeding. He'd probably like for William to be descended from Man o' War or some other famous race horse. Personally, I think you ought to be what you make yourself, not what you're born. So what if William doesn't have a lot of fancy ancestors. He's plenty smart! Just wait until the show; then everybody will see how smart he is!

Chapter 8

ON THE MORNING of the show, I dressed in a hurry because I'd laid out my clothes the night before and polished my boots and done everything, like even washing my hair. I wish my hair were long enough for braids. I had to pull it into pony tails and put rubber bands around them. Horsewomen aren't supposed to have hair flying all over the place. They aren't supposed to be sloppy in any way. The last thing I did was put on my favorite yellow neckband, the one like Tiffany's.

Daddy was drinking his coffee when I came into the kitchen. "Well, look at you!" he said, beaming. "My! How stylish Panky is becoming!"

Mother smiled, too. She's happy because I'm not so fat anymore.

"What would you like for breakfast?" she asked.

I said I couldn't eat a bite. All I could think about was the show.

"Not even one little egg?" said Mother. We compromised on a piece of toast, which I took with me in the car. Daddy drove me over, with Mother planning to come later.

When we got to Fox Run, I could feel the excitement as soon as I got out of the car. Some of the club members, grown people, dressed fit to kill, were trotting about the field, limbering up their horses. I began to get butterflies in my stomach.

We went to the office to get my number. I picked a round black card with a white number seven on it, and Daddy clipped it on the back of my jacket. I thought seven sounded lucky.

Then Daddy went outside to see what was going on, and I ran to get William. On our aisle, all you could smell was saddle soap and neat's-foot oil. Tiger Lily was clipped to cross-ties, and Tiffany was busy braiding her tail. I wished Tiffany would teach me to braid, but this wasn't a good time to ask.

Even if there were time, we were both too nervous.

William was already groomed, but I put more varnish on his hooves and gave him an extra lick with the dandy brush. He looked beautiful! His mane and tail felt like silk, and his coat shone with blue lights. I was glad Daddy had brought his camera. I wanted a picture of William looking like this to keep forever.

If only he would act as good as he looked. I showed him two carrots and said, "These are for you, IF you behave!"

I thought he got the idea.

After getting on at the mounting block, we headed for the outside pony ring to warm up. The field had about a hundred cars parked on it. Everybody in the club must have invited their friends and relatives. We had to pick our way through the crowd. William was sort of prancing and tossing his head. I was afraid it was my fault. Horses know when you're nervous. My legs felt stiff as boards, and I could feel myself yanking on the reins for no reason at all. The thing was, I could FEEL people looking at me in a critical sort of way. Here and there were a few familiar faces: Nicky Nickerson from my class at school, and Mrs. Horner, Caroline's mother. Then I saw Melanie leading Cupcake out of the stable. Cupcake was peering anxiously out from under a jaunty bow. It looked as if a butterfly had settled down in his forelock to take a rest. Melanie waved, but I didn't wave back. I needed both hands for William.

We managed to make it to the pony ring without anything happening. Katie was already there riding Caroline's Dixie. I didn't even recognize her at first. She was all dressed up in Caroline's jacket and helmet, and she must have covered up her freckles with make-up. She looked beautiful!

"Caroline's sick," she explained.

I didn't have to ask what with. I was having a mild attack of the same thing. My mouth was so dry, I could hardly swallow.

"Her mother asked me to ride Dixie," said Katie. She grinned, looking like her old self again.

Dixie was taking dainty, Thoroughbred steps as if she knew how elegant she looked. I hoped Caroline was far away somewhere. If she could see how good Katie looked on Dixie, she'd shoot herself.

"Dixie's a different horse when you ride her," I said, trying to keep the jitters out of my voice.

"Not everybody can ride a Thoroughbred," said Katie. "They're very sensitive. The things you could do on Boris would be like shouting at Dixie. All you have to do on her is think and she reacts!"

I had problems of my own. William had taken a dislike to his bit and was trying to spit it out. He rolled his jaw around testily, as if he'd swallowed his tongue and couldn't get it back up again. It was the same old bit he always used, so I knew nothing was wrong. I tried to keep a firm contact with his mouth, the way Hugo had told me, but I must have pulled too hard. William responded by walking sideways.

"Drive him forward with your legs," said Katie.

I did and William broke into a canter, one that threatened to turn into a flat-out gallop. I tried to rein him in, and we bounced unsteadily around the ring. As we whipped past Katie, William took a bite of air in Dixie's direction.

"Turn him in circles," said Katie.

I did, and it helped.

"Let's walk together," said Katie, looking worried.

I managed to hold William to a walk, but he took two steps to Dixie's one. It was embarrassing! Here Katie was, riding the flakiest horse in the stable, and she and Dixie were calming us down.

Just then, I heard my name being called over the loudspeaker.

"Good luck!" said Katie.

I directed William to the show ring, praying he wouldn't disgrace me. Daddy was waiting to hold the gate open for us.

He smiled reassuringly. "You're a good sport, Panky," he said. "Remember, this is just for the experience. It's fun!"

I managed a weak smile.

Tiffany and Tiger Lily came in next. They looked marvelous! Tiffany's blonde hair was braided and tied with a green ribbon. Tiger's tail was braided and tied with a matching bow. I knew nobody would look at me with them in the ring!

Actually, the big excitement was when Katie entered the ring on Dixie. You know in those old stories about knights, there was always a mystery knight showing up at the last minute and everybody started guessing who it might be. That's the way it was when Katie came in. You could almost hear invisible trumpets blowing!

There were two older girls competing in our class, but I didn't know who they were. They didn't look as good as Katie and Tiffany.

We walked around the ring, and it was like class except that about a million eyes were watching every move.

"Trot, please," a gravelly voice came over the microphone.

William surged ahead. Due to nervousness, he was trying to pass all the other horses. We had a private tug-of-war that I hoped didn't show, and I managed to hold him in place.

We cantered next, and I knew we looked good. Nobody has a better canter than William, not even Tiger Lily! I started feeling better.

The judge ordered us to line up for the awards, and I tried to keep William quiet by turning to stone myself. I didn't dare look to right or left, so I didn't know how anybody else was doing.

I heard the judge awarding first prize to Katie. I was surprised, but I shouldn't have been. Katie's very casual about competing. I think she competes with herself, to see if she can do better. If she hadn't been so modest, or maybe if she'd just been rich enough to dress up, I would have known how good she was.

Tiffany won second place. I didn't want to see her face. Out of the corner of my eye, I could see her going forward to collect her ribbon. That's when William decided he'd had enough.

Before I knew what he was doing, he

had torn out of line and was racing towards the judge. My helmet flew off, and I could hear people laughing. It must have been easy to see that William wanted his share of whatever was being handed out! I wrestled him back in line just in time to hear our names being called.

"Panky Mooney on William!"

This time, William marched forward like a perfect gentleman. He came to a halt, with his head high, ears stiffly forward, and his legs motionless as the judge awarded us

a pink ribbon for Most Improved Horse and Rider. I was really proud of William! He didn't bat an eye when the judge clipped the rosette on the side of his bridle. You'd think he had ribbons pinned on him every day of his life!

I could hear Daddy clapping louder than anybody else, and I looked around and saw Mother sort of misty-eyed. I hoped Hugo was watching.

When we left the ring, Daddy made us pose for a picture.

I'm usually self-conscious about having my picture taken, but this time I didn't mind. Our wonderful ribbon stood out against William's dark coat like a small pink flag!

Back in the stall, William put on a meek act. He tried to stick his nose in my pocket for a lump of sugar. I gave it to him and felt his soft muzzle tickle my hand.

"You were great, William," I whispered.

I was bending over to pick out his hooves when I heard Tiffany's mother. She was talking low, but she was furious.

"I don't want any excuses," she said. "Anybody can be a good loser. What I want is a good winner!"

I didn't move.

"We paid a fortune for that horse," she said, "plus heaven knows what for everything else. Why, I could buy a small town in India for what those lessons cost me!"

"I have to rub down Tiger," said Tiffany, in a small voice.

"Well, you go ahead and muck out or whatever it is you do," said her mother coldly. "I'm going out to watch the winners."

When I didn't think I'd be noticed, I crept out of William's stall and around the corner to the other aisle. I saw Katie putting Dixie away.

"Congratulations," I whispered.

"Thanks," said Katie. "The same to you! But why are you whispering?"

I told her what I'd overheard.

"That's too bad," she said. "I feel sorry for Tiffany."

"I wonder what Hugo would think," I said. "He tries to teach us sportsmanship."

"He should have a class for parents," said Katie.

She pinned the blue rosette on Dixie's gate.

"This is for Caroline," she said. "I'll be glad when she can have fun on her own horse."

I knew she meant it. Katie doesn't have to try to be a good sport. She just naturally is.

On the way out, I ran into Hugo. He stood, blocking my path, with his hands on his hips. He had sort of an inscrutable expression on his face. He was probably thinking William looked pretty silly when he tore out of line.

"Well, I'll bet it isn't the first time in history a horse tried to grab a ribbon," I blurted out. "It's normal when you think about it. People in this club certainly ought to think so. They care plenty about winning ribbons!"

Hugo threw his head back and roared. I had to laugh, too. Then Hugo stuck out his hand and shook mine.

"There'll be no holding him now that he's won a ribbon," he said. "William's a born competitor!" Then he got serious and looked me straight in the eye. "Congratulations, Panky!" he said. "You both deserved it!"

We did too. And next time, we'll do even better because we won't be so nervous.

I gave the ribbon to Mother. It was the first time in my life I'd ever won anything. Mother folded the ribbon with care and put it away in her pocketbook.

"You and William looked marvelous!" she said, proudly.

Chapter 9

I WISH I OWNED WILLIAM! Then I could buy him things like Tiffany does for Tiger Lily and Melanie does for Cupcake. Tiger has her own special saddle soap and her own grooming combs and brushes. She has three blankets, even a purple fishnet thing for summer called a 'cooling' blanket. Sometimes, I think everybody in the world is rich but me.

This afternoon, when Tiffany and I were putting away our horses, she said, "Tiger's blanket is awful! I ought to have it cleaned. Mother would scream if I bought a new one. This one's only six weeks old, but look at it!"

I looked. It had a few smudges on it, but I wouldn't have minded using it on my own bed. Then I looked at William's blanket. It was so crusted with dirt and mud, you couldn't see the plaid. I snatched it off his back, sending up a cloud of dust.

"This one's going to the cleaner's," I said, "if it doesn't cost too much."

Right away, I was sorry I'd mentioned cost. Tiffany doesn't talk about money, unless she's showing off about what she's buying next.

"Horse blankets are supposed to be washable," she said, "if you have a washing machine."

"Of course we have a washing machine!" I said, sounding angrier than I'd intended.

I found an old blanket in the tack room, even grubbier than the one William usually wears, and threw it over him. I folded the other one and when Mother came to pick me up, I sneaked it into the car, putting it on the floor against the front seat. Mother had been talking to Miss B, so she didn't notice.

On the way home, she said, "What is that awful smell, Panky? You seem to have brought the stable home with you."

"It must be my sweater," I lied. "This is the only one I have that fits under my jacket. I sure wish I had a new one."

This set Mother off.

"We need to cut back, Panky," she said. "You know that. This whole riding thing has gotten out of hand."

I felt like saying when it came to money, I was downright pathetic compared to everybody else; but I didn't. I didn't want a big row.

When Mother was busy in another part of the house, I dragged William's blanket around to the laundry room and stuffed it in the washing machine. I know I punched all the right buttons because I've watched Mother dozens of times.

The washer worked OK until spin-dry. Then it set off a screeching sound followed by heavy thumps. Finally, it spun to dead silence.

Mother came running.

"What was that noise?" she said, flinging open the lid of the washer.

I have to admit the smell was awful, but

the way Mother carried on, you'd think I'd stuffed a dead cat in the washer.

"Panky! Is this your doing?" said Mother.

I explained I was trying to save money by washing William's blanket instead of having it cleaned. Mother wouldn't even discuss it until she had shut the door of the laundry room.

"I wanted you to have a nice hobby," she said, "but horses aren't a hobby with you. They're an obsession!"

When Daddy came home, she hardly let him put his briefcase down before she started complaining.

"Panky has ruined my washer!" she said. "Right now, it's sitting out there with some evil-smelling horse thing in it and the filthiest water I've every seen!"

She gave Daddy time to take off his coat.

"And she says she was trying to save money!" Mother added.

Daddy usually sticks up for me. Tonight, he decided to take the blame.

"It's all my fault," he said, wearily. "I

plopped my family down in one of the richest counties in one of the richest states in the
union and expect them not to notice."

"But we couldn't live in the city,"
Mother protested.

"No, we couldn't," said Daddy. "I
wanted Panky to go to good schools and be
able to walk the streets in safety."

"And she can," said Mother.

"Still, it must be tough on her," said
Daddy, "not to be able to keep up with her
friends."

Mother wasn't about to give in.

"Nonsense!" she said. "There's a whole,
great big world out there that's not rich, and
Panky may as well start learning how to get
along in it!"

She added hastily, "Not that we're
poor. You got a lovely promotion when we
moved here."

Daddy hesitated.

"I'm not sure it was a promotion," he
said.

"What do you mean?" Mother's voice
was sharp. "Aren't you a vice-president?"

"That's my title," said Daddy, "but they

keep firing people. I'm still doing my old job, plus a new one."

I knew Mother wouldn't like hearing this. She enjoys telling people Daddy is vice-president of a steel company. It sounds pretty good.

"Oh, well," she said. "At least, you're not one of the ones being fired."

Daddy didn't answer.

I told myself I didn't have to worry. Daddy's smart, and nice, too. They'd be crazy to fire Daddy!

I tried not to think about it. I don't see other kids worrying about money all the time. Sometimes, things aren't so great around this house!

Chapter 10

IT WAS SATURDAY, and Daddy was driving me over to Fox Run. In my lap was William's neatly folded blanket. I hoped nobody would notice that it had shrunk to a size smaller and that the leather straps were sort of chewed up. Anyway, it smelled a lot better. Mother said next time I should take it to a washing machine place where the machines were bigger, and wash it in cold water. That's about all the talking to me she's done since yesterday. She's still mad, even though all that was wrong with her precious washing machine was a blown-out fuse.

"Today's March tenth," said Daddy. "Does that mean anything to you?"

"Oh," I said. "I forgot." It was my birthday, but I'd forgotten because Mother and I had agreed to wait until nice weather to have my party. Some birthday!

"Well, I didn't forget," said Daddy. "What would you like for a present?"

Due to the crumby state of the family finances, I tried to think small. All I could come up with was a new neckband.

"Is that all?" said Daddy. "Isn't there anything else?"

"Not a thing," I said.

Daddy gave me a look that said he knew better. I thought I'd better tell the truth.

"When I grow up," I said, "maybe I can afford a horse. If I'm lucky, William will still be alive and I can buy him. Horses live a long time if you take care of them."

"William?" said Daddy. "Is he that little black horse you rode in the show?"

I was amazed! It seems to me all I talk about is William, and Daddy wasn't even sure of his name!

Daddy stayed to watch the lesson, something he doesn't usually do. When the lesson was over and I was cooling off William, I saw Daddy talking to Hugo. William and I made a few tight circles in their vicinity so I could hear.

"I can't afford a horse with fancy breeding," I heard Daddy say. "What about William?"

Hugo assumed an expression of disdain.

"He's from Chicago, out of boxcar," he said.

Then he saw Daddy was serious, and he added, "Of course, as a horse to begin on, Panky could do worse."

I pretended to concentrate on making William back up. I sawed the reins left and right in turn, the way I'd seen Katie do. William responded with a few half-hearted bucks. Then he fell back on the tried-and-true William formula. When in doubt, run. We went half the ring before I got him back to a walk. Daddy and Hugo were still talking.

"When she outgrows William," Hugo was saying, "she can trade him in on a better horse."

Never! I thought. I wouldn't outgrow

William if we lived to be a hundred years old!

While I was putting William away, Daddy came to tell me the good news.

"Happy Birthday, Panky!" he said. "William is all yours!"

"Oh, Daddy!" I said. "Thank you! Thank you with all my heart!"

I threw my arms around his neck and hugged him.

"I didn't think it was a good idea to wait until you were both old and gray," Daddy said, smiling.

I looked to see how William was taking this.

"You're my horse now," I said, stroking his neck. For some crazy reason, I was crying. I was the luckiest person in the world to get the one thing I really wanted.

"I'll never ask for anything else as long as I live!" I said.

And I meant it.

Katie says horses don't know whether you own them or not. Maybe they don't, but William knew I was happy, and that made him happy. He's put his trust in me to take good care of him, and I hope I never let him down.

So what if he's not perfect! I'm not either.

Word spread fast about me and William, and my standing in the club went up right away. Tiffany and Melanie started giving me tips on grooming and where to buy things. For the first time, they were treating me like a member!

Chapter 11

WHEN YOU OWN a horse, you're supposed to buy your own tack. Somehow, I couldn't bring myself to ask my parents to buy me anything else. Besides, Mother would faint if she knew how much a new saddle costs.

Hugo solved the problem by saying he'd be on the lookout for a second-hand saddle for me. He said it would be better than a new one because it would be all broken in. Meanwhile, I'm using the same old club saddle, even though it's so big. I slide all over the place in it.

While I've been worrying about buying tack, everybody else has been losing theirs. Sleepy Hollow had a thief. Pieces of equipment were being stolen right out from under our noses. Hugo left his dog in the stable at night for protection, but nobody ever heard him bark.

I could picture bandits in ski masks sneaking into the tack room at night and making their getaway in a car parked in the bushes. It scared me to think of it.

I figured if anybody caught the thief, it would be Melanie. She spends more time in the stable than anybody else. She does everything but eat and sleep at Fox Run!

I never thought it would be me.

It happened this way. One afternoon, I stayed late to clean out William's stall. I needed a shovel, so I went to the tack room to look for one. I wasn't making much noise, for no special reason except that sometimes when things are real quiet, you find yourself acting quiet, too.

Anyway, when I stepped into the tack room, there was Tiffany. Something about the way she was standing struck me as odd. She was concentrating hard on removing a bit from a bridle. I stood in the doorway without saying anything.

Tiffany got the bit loose and shoved it into her pocket. That's when she saw me.

"Panky!" she exploded. "What do you mean sneaking up on me like that!"

I almost felt ashamed. Tiffany acted like a queen or something, outraged at the behavior of a lowly servant.

"I suppose you think I'm stealing!" Tiffany said angrily. "Well, how do you know this isn't mine?"

She was standing right under Melanie's peg with Cupcake's saddle and name printed over it on the wall.

Tiffany saw my glance.

"All right!" she said, fiercely. "So what if it is Melanie's bit. It's just an old bit! Now, I suppose you're going to run and tell Hugo."

I felt kind of sick.

"You've always been jealous of me!" Tiffany stormed.

I admired Tiffany more than anybody I knew. I wanted to be exactly like her. Was that being jealous? Oh, sure, maybe I had been a little jealous of the way she could buy things for Tiger.

"Well, what are you going to do?" she said, sounding less angry.

"What are YOU going to do?" I said, finally.

That caught her by surprise.

"I don't want Hugo to know," she said, "or my mother." All the fight was gone.

"Then you have to put back everything you've taken," I said. Tiffany thought it over.

"You mean you won't tell?"

"Not if you put everything back," I answered.

"I will, Panky," Tiffany said, "If you promise not to tell!"

I promised.

Somehow, it didn't seem over.

"I still admire you, Tiffany," I said.

"You do?" Tiffany sounded almost timid. "Whatever for? Katie's a better rider."

I tried to think of something.

"You're still trying to be a better rider," I said, "even if you don't win all the time."

"Thank you, Panky!" Tiffany's voice was almost a whisper. "I will! I'll put back everything I took."

I pretended to be busy looking for the shovel. I didn't want to see Tiffany crying.

In a few days' time, all the stolen items had been returned. Even things people thought they had lost out of carelessness turned up. I tried not to talk about it much because I was afraid it might show that I knew something. But I could tell, nobody suspected Tiffany was the thief. Everybody thought it was a groom or somebody who needed the money. Tiffany was the last person in the world you'd think of.

Hugo was the only one who didn't have anything to say. I think he suspected it was somebody in the club. His dog would have barked at an outsider.

Just when everybody had calmed down, Tiffany blew it. She got caught stealing from a local store. Thank goodness they didn't put her in jail like a criminal! She got sent to a psychiatrist instead, and she has to see him every week.

I've been doing a lot of thinking since this happened.

What is Tiffany really like? I thought

she had everything. But I was wrong. The reason somebody steals is because they don't have enough or they THINK they don't have enough! Tiffany has a beautiful horse and expensive clothes and everything anybody could want. I couldn't figure it out!

I remembered the way I used to hide candy and cake in my room to eat all by myself. I wanted whole cakes and pies, and I never got enough to eat. Was that so different from stealing?

Life was a lot simpler when all I wanted was to be like somebody else. Now, I've started asking questions, and I can't stop.

What am I like? Am I just somebody who wants to be like Tiffany?

I'd like to get inside this brain of mine. Is it an anxious brain? Is it a smart brain? What makes me the way I am?

I know one thing, I'm turning into a very selfish person. My family's worried sick about money, but all I've been thinking about is me and William and what I want to buy next!

Chapter 12

"HAVE YOU NOTICED something funny about Tiffany?" said Katie. "She hardly ever talks anymore."

I'd noticed all right, but I didn't dare say anything because I knew too much. Nobody but me knew Tiffany had been Fox Run's thief.

"That's right," I said, as if I hadn't thought of it before.

"I think I know what the trouble is," said Katie, keeping her voice low. We were in the stable, and you never knew who might have been listening. "Tiffany's been depressed ever since she didn't win first prize at the club show!"

I thought back. Maybe it had started then.

"But she's still taking lessons," I pointed out. "And I heard her asking about trying out for the MacClay."

"But her heart's not in it," said Katie. "The trouble is, she's too keyed up about winning! Of course, that's partly her mother's fault. She's a maniac about winning. What Tiffany needs is to relax and enjoy herself. There's more to riding than competition."

I couldn't answer that one. I'm pretty competitive myself. The difference between me and Tiffany was that she was way ahead of me.

"Let's invite Tiffany to go on a trail ride this afternoon," said Katie. "You can't think about competing when you're on the trail!"

"Today?" I asked in surprise. It was late March, and there were still patches of snow lying around in the shade.

"Sure!" said Katie. "We'll be OK as long as there's no ice."

I knew William would love the trail. It would be an adventure just for him to get out of the barn. I started getting excited.

"I'll take Boris," said Katie, "so we can swap horses if William gets too strong."

I ran to tack up William, and Katie went to tell Tiffany.

We met about twenty minutes later outside the barn. The sun was out, and it didn't feel too cold. There had been a rain the night before, and the scraggly bushes next to the barn sparkled with drops of water. The horses sniffed the air and pawed the ground with excitement.

"I'll lead on Boris," said Katie. "Panky, you follow on William, and Tiffany, you and Tiger can be last."

I thought the middle was a good place for William. If he was overcome with his usual desire to lead the parade, he'd bump smack into Boris.

"Keep a good grip with your legs," Katie said. "Remember what Hugo said about making a vise of your legs in case your horse gets spooked."

We waited by the horse crossing sign for a lull in traffic before hurrying across the highway. The trail led down a little hill and through some woods. The ground was mushy, but that was good because it slowed William down. As it was, he kept crashing into Boris's rear, and I knew he wasn't above nipping at Boris's hide.

Katie held up her hand for us to halt.

"Panky, you've got to hold William back!" she said. "Boris is good-natured, but he'll only take so much of having William crowd him! If you don't watch out, he's going to kick the daylights out of him!"

After that, when William got too close to Boris, I checked him by using a trick Hugo had taught me in class. I snatched my right rein up high, sort of putting on the brakes with little jerks. William did his share of pulling in return. I had to loop the rein around my right hand to keep a firm grip. After a little of this tug-of-war, William could see he wasn't getting anywhere, so he came up with a trick of his own. He gradually let his head come up until the reins were very short. Then he would savagely swing his head down so fast, it almost toppled me out of the saddle. I figured he'd settle down after a while, and I didn't want to change horses unless I had to. William couldn't run away because Boris plodded along in front of us, blocking the path.

Even with William full of mischief, it was fun to be outside. The woods were pretty, in a winterish sort of way. The tree limbs were tangled lavender against a silver sky. Here and there, bushes with red berries brightened things up. And when you're on a horse, you notice smell. The woods smelled damp, like dug-up roots and worms coming out of the ground and piles of wet old leaves.

I looked around at Tiffany. She was noticing things, too. She and Tiger were swinging their heads around, sniffing and looking.

We came to Talmadge Hill Station where Daddy catches the train to the city.

Katie said, "I made sure we'd go past the station when there were no trains. I didn't want William spooked his first time out."

I was sure glad she'd thought of that. A train makes a lot of noise, snorting and puffing and grinding to a stop. Even when you know what it is, it's scary!

"I'm not sure Tiger's used to trains either," said Tiffany, but she didn't look worried. In fact, she looked happier than I'd seen her for a long time!

The best part of the trail was a big estate that had been given to the town of Old Forge. I'd been there before for kite-flying contests and Fourth of July contests. There were big fields and some woods and an old house. Katie said we'd better stick to the trail in the woods because the open field might make William bolt.

We ambled along past a pond with ducks on it, and it was nice and peaceful when all of a sudden, William stopped dead in his tracks. I flopped over on his neck. Then he took a few rapid steps backwards, his muscles bunched up with panic. By the side of the trail, I could see some reddish brown fur showing through a bush. The creature leaped into our path. It was a deer, a beautiful, sleek creature staring at us with great, startled eyes. We were so close, I

could see his eyelashes. They were long and silky, like Bambi's.

The deer held us for a second with his wide-eyed stare, then bounded away. At almost the same moment, William bucked me off so fast, I didn't know what had happened. I looked up from the ground, breathless, to see him trotting off without me!

Katie tried to grab his reins, but that only made him go faster.

"William! Ho!" I called, using my best command voice.

William turned his head and gave me a long, thoughtful look. I took a step forward. So did he. I walked faster, and William picked up a trot. No matter what I did, William kept an even pace ahead of me. He kept checking to see if I was still there, but he wasn't about to let me catch up.

Katie offered me a ride behind her on Boris, but I refused because I wanted to grab William's reins if I could.

When William got to the highway, I held my breath. He paused, looked in both directions, then trotted across. I heard the clattering of his hooves on the pavement and then quiet as he got to the field.

I heaved a sigh of relief. He was safe!

Now, I had a new worry. How was it going to look to have William trotting up without me? Everybody knows you're supposed to hold on to a horse's reins, no matter what. Even if I'd done three flips in the air, I was supposed to hold on to the reins. This was going to be embarrassing!

We found William standing by his stall. Luckily, the grooms were out, and no one had seen him trot up without me. I wasted no time getting him into his stall, turning him to face the gate before removing his saddle and slipping off his bridle. Tiffany and Katie dismounted and watched me. Boris and Tiger stood as calm as a couple of old sheep. They hadn't given a second's trouble. I started to get mad.

"William certainly didn't act very loyal!" I said.

Tiffany and Katie tried to look sympathetic.

"He's not Black Beauty," said Katie, "but

he did keep checking to see if you were all right."

I felt awful! It was all right to have people laugh at me in the beginning, but now I was supposed to be a fairly good rider.

"Do you promise not to tell a living soul what happened?" I said.

"We promise!" they chorused.

"As far as we're concerned, this never happened," Katie said solemnly.

Tiffany made a choking sound, and the next thing we knew, we were giggling our heads off. Tiffany laughed so hard, she had tears streaming down her face.

I couldn't even stay mad at William. He wouldn't be half as much fun if he were dull and dependable like Boris.

I wish the day had ended right there, with all of us laughing and Tiffany looking happy, but there was another surprise ahead for me—and not a nice one either.

Chapter 13

WHEN MOTHER drove me home from Fox Run, we found Daddy's car already parked in the driveway. It was only five-thirty and he doesn't usually get home until seven. Neither of us said anything, but I think we knew something was wrong.

Daddy gave us the bad news right away. He'd been fired.

After he told us, he sat down suddenly, as if he couldn't take anymore. Mother went over and put her arms around him.

"Panky and I will LOVE having you home for a while!" she said, trying to sound cheerful.

He lowered his head into his hands, the picture of defeat.

"We appreciate you!" Mother said.

I had to give her credit. She must have felt like yelling. To tell the truth, I didn't feel so good myself. My mind raced ahead to awful possibilities. How do you buy groceries when there's no money? And what about me and William? What was going to become of us?

After that, Daddy stayed home. He got up early every morning, as if he were going to work, but then he just sat around. Sometimes, he read help wanted ads in the paper. Other times, he worked on his resumé. The purpose of a resumé is to tell people how great you are so they'll want to hire you. Only Daddy didn't think he was great. He said things like, "Anybody have a job for a middle-aged executive on the way down?" And Mother would say, "Don't talk that way in front of Panky."

In the afternoons, Daddy got in the habit of cutting logs and stacking them. He kept a fire going in the living room, and he turned the thermostat way down to save on oil. Every room in the house got to be freezing except the living room.

On Saturday, the day Daddy used to always run errands, he said, "How about going into the village with me, Panky?"

I said, OK, even though I didn't especially want to.

We went to the hardware store, which is practically Daddy's favorite place in the world. He bought little wire cups, shaped like a king's crown.

"The people who sold us this house," he said, "would have saved me a lot of trouble if they'd put these on in the first place."

I didn't ask why.

"When you put these on top of the drain pipes," Daddy explained anyway, "they keep the leaves from clogging them up."

I didn't put on a big act of being interested, and after a while, he said, "How are you and William getting along?"

"Terrific!" I said. "Even Hugo says William is learning. He says it shows you can teach a calf if you work at it!"

Daddy laughed. "Hugo's a snob about breeding, but that dog of his is quite a mixture."

Hugo's dog is part Shepherd and part I don't know what else. He has three legs because a horse stepped on him when he was a puppy. He's really funny looking, but Hugo doesn't hold that against him. You can always tell when Hugo is around because you see his dog.

Anyway, I was glad to hear Daddy laugh.

"Last week, Katie and Tiffany and I went out on the trail," I said. "We saw a deer."

I didn't say anything about falling off.

"It was beautiful!" I said. I wish Daddy could ride! The world looks so much better when you're on the back of a horse.

"Our trail goes right by your station," I said. "You know, the station you used to commute from."

"Come to think of it," said Daddy. "I've seen horses out of the train window. Hey! What do you do if a train scares your horse?"

I had the answer because Katie had told me.

"If a train spooks your horse," I said,

"turn him to face the train so he gets a good look at it."

Daddy laughed. "And then he won't be scared?" he said.

I wasn't too crazy about the idea myself. Knowing William, he'd be halfway back to the stable before the train had gone by.

It didn't matter. I was glad to hear Daddy laughing. He sounded like his old self, good-natured and ready to see a joke. I can't figure out why anybody would fire somebody like Daddy. He's smart and nice and a hard worker too. It would be different if he were a crook or something.

"Daddy, why did they fire you?" I said.

Daddy's good humor vanished.

He cleared his throat.

"As you know," he said, "the steel business is in a great deal of trouble. We've had to close down several plants, and there were too many workers. They didn't need me anymore."

I still didn't understand. His company hadn't fired everybody, so why had they fired Daddy? It didn't make sense, but I didn't think I'd better say anything else.

When we got home, Daddy lowered the thermostat and put more logs on the fire. Flames leaped up like a bonfire!

Mother poked her head out of the kitchen.

"Not too big," she said, "unless you plan to stay with it."

"I'll watch the fire," I said. Daddy's always starting fires and not staying with them, and Mother's always worrying about sparks setting the house on fire.

"There's something I want to talk to you about," Daddy said, following Mother into the kitchen. "How would you like to have a wood stove?"

I could tell by the way Mother was banging pots and pans that she didn't like the idea. I've noticed a funny thing. When Daddy acts cheerful, Mother gets down in the dumps. And when Daddy is really sunk, Mother brightens up.

"Listen!" said Mother.

I peeked in the kitchen. A line like an

exclamation point appeared between Mother's brows. She held up her hand.

"Can you hear it?" said Mother.

There was a dull, clanking sound.

"It's the well," said Mother. "We're running out of water!

We listened.

"Everybody around here has an artesian well," said Mother. "At first, the pump clanked when I did the wash. Then it clanked for any little thing, like flushing the toilet."

Daddy's shoulders drooped, all his good humor gone.

"Come to think of it," he said, "I did notice the pressure was down."

"I've known for weeks," said Mother, "but I didn't want to worry you. The plumber says we need a new well."

She allowed Daddy a few seconds to take in this new calamity. Then she said, "He said it would be hard to find water because we're on a hill. He said we might consider using a dowser."

Daddy suddenly came to life.

"A dowser!" he shouted. "You mean one of those people who prowls around with a forked stick?"

"Yes," said Mother, almost cheerfully. "And when the stick twitches, that means they're standing over water!"

"Why, that's right out of the middle ages!" said Daddy. "We might as well call in our friendly, neighborhood witch!"

"If you're going to be unreasonable, we can't talk," said Mother.

"Unreasonable? Who's unreasonable?!" shouted Daddy.

This was shaping into a major fight, the kind I didn't want to hear. I left the fire and went into a cold room to watch television. Their voices followed me.

"I've always felt you had a lot of untapped executive ability," I heard Daddy say sarcastically. "It's really wasted on Panky and me."

I wished he would leave me out of it. So Mother was bossy! He wasn't perfect either.

I tried to concentrate on TV. It was

some dumb comedian, and everything he said was followed by this phony roar of laughter. It was probably canned laughter of people long since dead and gone. I didn't feel like laughing along with them.

I turned off the set. I needed to think. My family was falling apart. I would have to be deaf, dumb, and blind not to notice.

I wished everything were different. I wished Mother and Daddy didn't fight and that we were rich and that I didn't have to worry about the future of the steel business. I almost felt sorry for myself, but I've been around Katie too much for that. Like it or not, these were my problems, too. What it came to was this: How long could I go on spending money keeping a horse and having lessons when my father was out of a job?

Chapter 14

MISS B SAYS all horses feel is "cupboard love" and the reason they make a fuss when they hear you coming is that they want the tidbits you bring them. I don't believe that. Oh, sure! William is nuts about a carrot or an apple; but I know, in his own way, he loves me. We have a true understanding.

Today, I brushed him an extra long time and sang, "My Bonnie Lies Over the Ocean." William kept one ear flicked back, listening.

I wondered how long I'd be able to keep on riding. Fox Run costs money. I don't know exactly how much, but with Daddy out of a job, it was probably more than we could afford.

William sensed my mood, I could tell.

"No matter what," I told him. "I still love you. Wherever you go in this wide world, you'll always be my little horse."

For some reason, I started crying. I wiped my eyes on his mane. If I stayed, I knew I'd start blubbering, so I ran to watch whatever was going on in the ring.

I ran smack into Melanie and Cupcake. Melanie had Cupcake tied to tethering rings as if he were some kind of wild animal. They were taking up the whole aisle. Cupcake's hair lay around them like snow.

"Melanie!" I said, hastily wiping my eyes. "Don't you ever go home?"

"This is my home," said Melanie, running a comb through Cupcake's tail. "By the way, I've got some great oil for hooves. It has something in it that helps prevent thrush. In case you didn't know it, that's something we have to watch out for."

"Oh, sure," I said. "Thanks for the information."

I think it sounded sarcastic, but I didn't care. Melanie knows a lot, but she can really get on your nerves the way she lays it on you. Katie waits until you ask.

I stepped around Cupcake's shiny little hooves and made my way down the aisle.

Tiffany had been watching from Tiger's stall.

"It's sad," she said, when I reached her. She kept her voice low so Melanie wouldn't hear.

"She's too big for Cupcake, and she can't bring herself to sell him."

I almost felt sorry for Melanie. I knew I'd feel the same way about William.

"Cupcake's OK for a little kid," said Tiffany, "but imagine him trying to keep up with us in class!"

I could picture Cupcake trotting furiously to keep up with William, and I knew it wouldn't work. It was too bad.

I found Katie watching a lesson, and I sat down beside her.

"Melanie's 'pulling' Cupcake," I said. "Isn't that what you call it when you pull hair out with a comb?"

"Yes," said Katie. "Melanie's good at it, but I'm surprised Cupcake has any hair left to pull. He gets groomed almost every day."

"It's sad," I said, echoing Tiffany's words.

"Yes, it is," said Katie. "I understand her mother's been under the weather for several weeks."

I looked surprised.

"Oh," said Katie. "I thought you knew. Her mother has a drinking problem."

I was shocked. Poor Melanie! I guess everybody has problems.

"Sometimes, it's not so nice around

Melanie's house," said Katie. "Of course, I don't know much about it."

Katie doesn't like to gossip. She wouldn't have said anything if she hadn't thought I already knew.

I watched the lesson, but I was thinking of Melanie and the way she shut out problems at home and pretended they didn't exist. It must be awful to have a mother who drank too much! On the other hand, Melanie wasn't doing much to help by spending every hour of the day with Cupcake. It was as if her mother didn't even exist. I didn't want to be like that. My family was in trouble, and I wanted to help.

I realized then that there was only one thing for me to do. I had to give up William! Deep down, I think I'd known it all along.

With a heavy heart, I went back to William's stall. He had a straw hanging down from his forelock, the way he had the first time I saw him. I plucked the straw out and stroked his nose. If it hadn't been for me, Hugo might have gotten rid of William, and he'd be dog food by now.

I kissed William's wet, rubbery nose.

"Anybody would like you now," I said, "but, remember, I'm the one who liked you first."

Chapter 15

WHEN I WENT OVER to Fox Run today, all I could think of was how much I was going to miss the place. Inside the barn, little gray sparrows were making a big racket in the rafters, darting down to pick up straws for their nest and hurrying back. Hugo's dog was lying in a pile of straw to keep warm with just his head poking out. The whole place smelled of horses and hay; and, if you happen to like cats, and I do, Miss B's big tabby was about to have a litter of kittens. She was on the prowl now for mice, and her swollen stomach hung down to the floor. I leaned over and petted her. I wouldn't be around to see the kittens.

Melanie passed by, taking Cupcake out

for a stroll. Cupcake was snugly buckled into his blue plaid blanket for his outing.

"How's William today?" said Melanie.

"OK, I guess," I answered. "How's Cupcake?"

"He's excited about going outside," said Melanie. "See him sniffing the air? He's been off his feed lately, and this is just what he needs to perk him up."

I like the way at Fox Run, when you meet people, they don't say, "How are you?" and you say, "fine", and that's the end of it. Over here, people always say, "How's William?" and you tell them, and you ask about their horse, and they tell you, and all of a sudden, you've had an interesting conversation. Honestly, I don't know what I talked about before joining Fox Run. It couldn't have been very interesting.

I tacked up William, thinking how lucky I'd been to own my own horse, even for a little while. It had been dumb of me to wish for cashmere sweaters or expensive new equipment. Just owning William should have been enough.

Katie and I decided to go out on the trail. We didn't talk until we got to the woods. Then Katie turned in her saddle to face me.

"Maybe you can hunt next fall," she said. "At the rate William is improving, he might be ready."

I didn't say anything.

"Of course, Hugo may insist that you ride Boris the first time out," she continued, "just to be on the safe side."

I looked at the bare trees. Winter's ugly for most people, and when I stopped riding, it was going to start being ugly for me again.

"If you're nervous," Katie said, "you can start out by cubbing. That's for green horses and riders, and you can drop out if you get scared. Of course, you and William will have to learn how to jump first, but you have six months to do that in."

I wondered how a person as kind-hearted as Katie could chase a poor, innocent fox and watch the hounds tear it to bits! Didn't anybody feel sorry for the fox?

Katie misunderstood my silence.

"Don't knock Boris," she said. "He may be a beginner horse, but he's GREAT in the hunt field. He can keep up with the best of them. And he's a good jumper, too."

I'd never told Katie my true feelings about hunting and I didn't see any point in doing it now.

"I don't think William would like hunting," I said. "He would probably dump me and try to lead the pack alone," I said.

Katie laughed.

"I can see him now, racing past every horse on the field! But you never know, Panky, how a horse will act until you get there. Take Dixie. She goes to pieces at the slightest thing in the ring, but on a hunt, she settles right down to business. Where we van the horses, there are miles and miles of empty fields," she rambled on happily. "It's all so beautiful! The pink coats, sleek, excited horses, the smell of dew in the field! And the hounds love it! When they get the scent, they start barking like crazy, and your horse takes off as if he's got wings!"

She was getting to the bad part.

"When the hounds corner the fox," she said, "we all gather around, and the hunt master holds up the fox's tail and we get blooded."

I shuddered.

"Just a nice friendly little scene!" I burst out. "Everybody gets smeared with blood!"

Katie pulled up her horse and looked at me with astonishment.

"I didn't know you felt that way, Panky. I thought everybody liked hunting!"

I came back at her with Mother's words.

"There's a whole great big world out there," I said, "and it's not all gung-ho for hunting!"

The look on Katie's face made me ashamed. It wasn't her fault about hunting. I tried to change the subject.

"You know what?" I said. "Hugo says you're the most talented horsewoman he's seen in a generation."

I remember I wished he'd said it about me.

"Why don't you enter more shows?" I said.

"Don't think I haven't thought about it,"

said Katie. "But I need a sponsor. The show circuit is expensive. You know what Hugo says, 'In this business you don't get much better than your horse.' I need a sponsor with a good horse who'll pay for vanning and entry fees and all the rest."

It was my turn to be surprised.

"Personally, I don't see what the sponsor gets out of it," Katie said. "They come to the big shows to share in the glory, but that's all. On the little shows, you call them, collect, to tell them the results, but that's all the fun they have."

Katie always makes the best of things. I had to start being that way, too.

I looked around me. The sun was going down, a big red ball behind tangled black tree limbs. I guess the deer was still out there somewhere, lurking in the brush, but I didn't care. I felt sad, as if I were miles and miles from home.

That night, Mother and Daddy had another argument about money. Daddy wanted to buy a chain saw, and Mother didn't want him to spend the money.

"A chain saw would save hours of my

labor," Daddy said, "but you probably think my time is worthless!"

"I know how hard you're trying," said Mother, "but I hate the thought of buying anything!"

Usually, when my parents have a fight, I cooperate by pretending to watch television. Tonight, I barged in on them.

"I just thought you'd like to know," I said. "I'm giving up William, so that's one expense you won't have!"

I didn't wait for them to say anything. I ran to my room, crying.

Chapter 16

I STAYED AWAY from Fox Run for a couple of days. Today, at school, Katie was waiting for me in the cafeteria. As soon as we sat down with our trays, she came to the point.

"Something's bothering you, Panky," she said. "Tell me what it is. Please!"

I decided to be as honest as she is.

"Daddy's lost his job, and I'm going to give up riding."

"Wow!" said Katie.

I felt better having it out in the open.

"That's really heavy!" said Katie.

I made an effort to chew my sandwich. I didn't want to cry in the lunchroom.

"But if you sell William," Katie said, "you're going to get really depressed!"

I knew she was right. I felt awful now, but I was going to feel a lot worse when William was gone.

"I sure hope you don't sell William," Katie said.

"But we don't have any money!" I said.

Katie and I are in a different position when it comes to horses. My lessons cost plenty, but Katie's are free because she's working and helping Hugo train horses.

"Listen, Panky," Katie said. "I know how William can earn his keep, if you're willing."

Her green eyes widened with excitement.

"You could rent him out for kids to use at birthday parties! Miss B says she's always getting calls from people wanting horses to use at parties. They want LITTLE horses, like William!"

Katie's words stuck in my mind. Later, when we were out on the trail, I was still thinking about what she said. It was nice of Katie to want to help out but I couldn't see it.

"You'd be there to lead him around and

protect him," said Katie watching me
closely. "And you could make money renting
him out to summer camps," she continued.

I wondered what was the good of owning your own horse if you had to share him
with everybody!

Katie could see I didn't like the idea.

"Well, it's better than losing him forever!" she said. "Think about it."

I thought about it for a few minutes.
She was right. It was a lot better!

"I'll do it," I said. "And if Daddy gets

another job, maybe I can afford to go back to having lessons."

I started feeling better. It would have been terrible to watch William being hauled away in a van, heading goodness knows where!

Katie suggested I put ads on the bulletin boards in supermarkets, saying Horse for Rent. She said to be sure to draw William's picture so everybody could see how cute he was.

When I got home from Fox Run, Daddy and Mother were waiting for me. Daddy had his usual bonfire going.

"Sit down, Panky," Daddy said. "Your mother and I want to talk to you."

I sat on a stool near the fire.

"We appreciate your willingness to give up William," said Daddy. "We know you were trying to help the family. We're all going to have to make sacrifices, but your mother and I completely agree about one thing. This is one sacrifice you won't have to make. William is a part of the family now, and he stays!"

I felt as if a great weight had lifted. I ran over and gave Daddy a hug.

Daddy turned me to face Mother.

"Now your mother has something to say."

Mother looked nervous. She doesn't like family scenes, even good ones.

"Panky, we keep forgetting that you're growing up," she said, sounding rehearsed. "I'm sure you must have heard some of the talk around the house and been worried."

That was putting it mildly.

"Well, I was sort of wondering what we'd eat," I said.

They laughed.

"You can stop worrying about that," said Mother, "because I've gotten a job as a cook. I'm going to be working at home, helping out a local cateress. We'll be cooking for wedding receptions and parties, and I'll have plenty of time to cook extra for us!"

I was amazed that Mother would do a thing like this. She's basically a snob, and this meant moving down the social ladder in a hurry.

"You showed a lot of spunk, Panky," Mother said. "I thought if you could do it, so could I!"

It was time to tell them Katie's suggestion.

"If you can bear sharing William," Daddy said, "it might be a big help."

"I figure things won't stay this way forever." I said.

"You bet they won't!" said Daddy.

After that, I went to my room to make an ad to hang in supermarkets. I drew a beautiful picture of William with a pink balloon tied to his tail!

Chapter 17

ONE NIGHT, after cooking hot dogs over the fire, Daddy suddenly announced, "I'd like to take my family out to the Bear Tooth Pass."

He lit his pipe and stared dreamily into the fire.

"We could fly to Billings, Montana, rent a car, and drive through the mountains. Panky, do you know why it's called the Bear Tooth Pass?"

I didn't know.

"Because the mountains look like bear's teeth," said Daddy.

"I was in Montana once," said Mother. "I remember driving along toward this big mountain, and no matter how many miles we went, we didn't get any closer to the mountain."

"It's big country," Daddy admitted, "but I think it's time this family saw something besides a hothouse suburb."

He leaned his head back and blew some shaggy lopsided O shapes into the air. "Come to think of it," he said, "it might not be a bad idea to settle out there."

"You mean leave Old Forge?" said Mother, sounding alarmed.

I burned my tongue on a marshmallow.

"Why not?" said Daddy. "Our roots here don't run very deep. Panky, how would you like to live out west?"

For some reason, I didn't like the idea.

"William would love Montana," said Daddy. "He probably came from somewhere out west."

Maybe he did, I thought, but he'd have to travel in a trailer or van, and he hates them! I could imagine him rocking along in a rickety trailer, getting carsick, staring at that lonesome mountain!

"We'd travel on the route of Lewis and Clark," Daddy said. "And be pioneers, the way they were. I like that."

He knocked his pipe ashes in a messy little heap, near, but not on, the hearth.

Mother pointedly looked at the ceiling. She's trying to hang loose, but she's not that loose.

"I knew a man once," she said, "who moved out west and made a living selling coffee tables made of tree slabs. They were full of knotholes and tree rings, and they had bark around the edges."

"I think I can do a little better than that," Daddy said, stiffly.

"Well, I don't know who would buy this house!" said Mother. "We won't find anybody as dumb as we were!"

"We'll just give it a coat of white paint and keep our mouths shut," said Daddy.

Mother laughed at that, and Daddy was so pleased, he turned pink.

And that's how it got decided we were going to move. Daddy kept on mailing out resumés, but I don't think he was very hopeful about things.

What I wished was that Daddy would get another job in the city. Then we'd stay right here. Somehow, I didn't like the idea of the Bear Tooth Pass. Daddy means well, but nothing he did was quite right, like building fires that were too big.

Daddy told me there were places in Montana where children rode their horses to school. I had to admit that would be neat! But I wondered if William would mind being tied all day to a rail outside a country school. Of course, he'd have company. I'll bet his coat would get so thick, he'd look like a buffalo!

Today, we had our tag sale at our house.

I did my share of the work beforehand by cleaning up my room and making a stack of old games and clothes. Then I stuck them out in the yard on a card table with a cheap price on them.

Mother had nailed paper plates to trees with Tag Sale, ten o'clock, printed on them in front of our house. By nine o'clock, there were cars all up and down Whiskey Lane and the people were getting out and hurrying to our yard.

Daddy and I stood by the window, peeking out at them. Mother hurried by with an old eggbeater.

"I imagine they have eggbeaters out west," she said.

We were going to travel light, even if all we did was move to the other side of town. There would be Daddy and Mother and William and me, and the bare essentials, things William couldn't do without, like the saddle Hugo found for me and one of Tiger's old blankets that Tiffany gave me.

"I'd better go write all this down in my journal," I said. "Nothing's turning out the way I expected."

Daddy looked sympathetic.

"I've heard life is something that happens to you when you're on your way to something else," he said.

I had to think about that one. I certainly hoped Daddy didn't start going in for wise sayings.

"Just think," said Daddy. "When we moved here, I had no idea a horse was going to be an important member of our family."

He turned away from the view of people pawing all our ash trays and flower vases and household junk.

"Out west," he said, "a man still has a little space left. Who knows? I might even decide to build us a log cabin!"

I didn't like any of this.

I went back to cleaning out closets. It seemed like a good time to throw things away.

Later, I heard Daddy telling Mother a corny joke, and Mother not laughing.

"You didn't have a sense of humor when we got married," Mother said, reproachfully.

"You're not laughing very hard right now," said Daddy.

"I'm worried," said Mother. "I don't know what's ahead."

I felt uneasy, as if Daddy were going to lead us into a strange Montana desert and leave us lost and starving, like the father in Hansel and Gretel.

There was a long silence.

"If you had it to do all over again," said Daddy, "would you still marry me?"

"Yes," said Mother, not hesitating. "What about you? I know I'm an old harpy about half the time. Would you still marry me?"

"You bet!" said Daddy. "Marrying you was the smartest thing I ever did!"

Things got quiet. I knew they were kissing, and I was glad. I don't think I realized until then how scared I'd been. Scared of being poor, scared of moving to a new place, scared of having nobody to take care of me! Now, I wasn't scared anymore!

I tossed a game of Monopoly on the floor, starting a new pile. William is the only thing of value I own, and he stays with us, no matter what happens!

Chapter 18

ALL THIS TIME, Daddy was mailing out resumés, but he didn't say much about it. It must have felt like sending out letters to Santa Claus.

Poor old Daddy! It looked as if nobody wanted him. That was why he dreamed of going out west where he'd be important and could take care of his family without needing so much money.

If anybody ought to understand, it was me. When I'd been fat and had no friends, I'd felt the same way. I used to dream about being a cowgirl and sitting around the camp-fire singing with friends who cared about me.

It must be terrible to be a grown man and feel worthless and unwanted. When you're little, you can tell yourself that you'll grow up some day and things won't hurt so much. What do you tell yourself when you're already grown?

One morning, after the tag sale, while we were waiting to sell our house, Daddy got up early and dressed carefully and caught the train to the city. When he came home late in the afternoon, he had bags of groceries with him.

"I swung by the village and did a little shopping," he said, dropping his bundles on the kitchen table.

His groceries turned out to be a big steak, a pound of butter, a long loaf of French bread, and a fabulous Black Forest cake, dripping with chocolate and cherries!

Mother eyed the cake critically.

"I happen to know where you bought that cake," she said; "and I could have made one just as good for one-third the cost."

She was too busy glaring at the cake to notice the look on Daddy's face.

"We don't have to worry about the expense," said Daddy, almost exploding with excitement. "You're looking at a working man!"

Mother let out a joyous whoop, and she

and Daddy danced around the table. Then they remembered me and included me in a big hug.

We had a feast that night, cooking the steak over the fire and eating off of the coffee table. Daddy turned up the thermostat, but we actually got too hot and had to turn it down. I think things have to get real bad before they can feel this good!

"Once a steel man, always a steel man!" Daddy said, proudly.

After supper, he said, "There's going to be a regular paycheck coming into this house from now on. That means you two girls can relax." He put his arm over mother's shoulder.

"You don't have to cook for other people's parties," he said. "You can join the Garden Club if you like."

Mother looked thoughtful.

"But I like my job," she said, "and in case you haven't noticed it, I'm turning into a darn good cook!"

"And I don't think William will mind giving little kids a ride at birthday parties," I said. "Not if I'm there to take care of him."

Daddy looked surprised.

"Well, I seem to have a couple of liberated women on my hands," he said.

There was one thing still bothering me, and I came out with it.

"Are we still trying to sell our house? I don't want to leave Old Forge," I said. "William and I are just beginning to be good, and I want to keep on having lessons with Hugo."

"I'd like to stay in Old Forge too," said Mother. "It's convenient for my job. But I want a house in the village with a little yard. I hate gardening!"

Daddy grinned.

"That's OK by me," he said. "I'll leave the house hunting to you. I'll be in the city every day."

So it looks as if I've heard the last of the Bear Tooth Pass, and I'm just as glad. I'd dreaded the thought of loading William into a trailer. Just the sight of a trailer shakes him up. Hugo says some horses are more afraid of moving then they are of dying. They must think wherever they are is better than where they might be going.

I'm kind of worried about one thing though. I think all my moods have been hard on William. Horses may not have intelligence, but they have INTUITION, and that's just as good. William didn't know what was going on, but he could sense my worry.

I talked it over with Katie, and she said why didn't we show William a little of the world, like where I live. That seemed like a good idea. For all William knows, the world drops off at the end of his familiar trail.

So one sunny day, when the air was warm and springlike, we saddled up the horses and rode all the way to my house. There was a big For Sale sign in the front yard. I stood by it and pointed William's head at the house and said, "See! This is where I live for now, but soon I'll be moving. When we get a new house, I'll take you to see it."

I will too, even if I have to ride him into the village and up on the sidewalks!

William gave our house his most intelligent stare. He could have been saying, "So this is where you are when you're not with

me." Then Katie and I let the horses eat grass, and Mother came out with a glass of lemonade for us. I let her give William a lump of sugar to make friends, but, honestly, she was so nervous, you'd think William was going to bite her arm off!

Summer is almost here, and there have been a lot of changes at Fox Run. Caroline's mother gave up on turning Caroline into a horsewoman and put Dixie up for sale. Caroline is thinking of taking ballet lessons, and she's so happy, she's a different person! She must have hated horses!

Hugo says it frequently happens that people who care about horses want their children to enjoy them too, only they don't. Then along comes somebody with a true love of horses and nobody knows where it came from. Like me!

Tiffany is still riding, and she's beginning to enjoy it in a new way. I don't know what her mother thinks, but Tiffany doesn't care about winning ribbons all the time, and that's good. It's good for her to go out on the trail with Katie and me. You don't think about competing when you're on the trail.

We have a lot of fun together. Sometimes, we pack a lunch and eat it in the woods.

The big news is Katie. There's a good chance she can win enough points at shows to be able to compete for the MacClay at the National Horse Show. And she doesn't have to worry about the expense because she's found a sponsor, a nice, friendly woman who's really interested in Katie and loves horses.

I'll probably be seeing Katie on TV, wearing a stock and a derby and looking like a million dollars.

The end of this journal was supposed to be about how William and I got to be famous, and instead it's going to be Katie!

The funny thing is, I don't mind.

Melanie is the only one who's exactly the same. I think she would go on grooming Cupcake if there were an earthquake!

Oh, I guess I ought to put in that I'm getting to be a pretty good rider. I may not be as good as Katie, or even as good as Tiffany, but I'm a real horsewoman, and I'm proud of it!

Hugo says next fall, he's going to start

a class in dressage, and he wants me and William in it! I can't wait! Hugo says dressage is horse language.

There hasn't been any talk about trading William in on a better horse. He's improving right along with me, just as I knew he would. He's probably going to be brilliant in dressage!

I've learned a lot since I started riding, and not just about horses. When I look back on that first day, I thought Tiffany was the exact model of what I wanted to be, and that Caroline was stuck-up, and that Melanie was a know-it-all, and that Katie was a terrible rider. I was wrong about everything! I found out that Caroline was scared stiff, Melanie was trying to cope in her own way with the problem of an alcoholic mother, and that Katie was by far the best rider at Fox Run. Tiffany was the biggest surprise of all. She had everything money could buy, but she got depressed because she couldn't be first all the time and started stealing! That was when I had to stop trying to be exactly like Tiffany and figure out who I was.

I'm me. I'm a person who was fat, and I'm not anymore. I'm not the best rider and I'm not the worst. But don't think I'm putting myself down. I'm a pretty good rider, and I'm getting better all the time.

When it comes to being a good sport, well—I'll have to work at that. I wasn't born that way, like Katie.

Horses are still the biggest thing in my life, but they're not the only thing. I love Mother and Daddy too and being part of a family.

But I'll always feel a special love for William because he's mine and I loved him before I was sure of anything else.